Izzy Gizmo

Pip Jones and Sara Ogilvie

London
Delhi

IZZY GIZMO, a girl who **LOVED** to invent,
carried her tool bag wherever she went
in case she discovered a thing to be mended,
or a gadget to tweak to make it more splendid.

But the trouble with things that have dials and switches is they don't always **work**, they have certain glitches.

The **Tea-Mendous**, for instance, did such a fine job . . .

Till out popped a piston and off dropped a knob!

Then the Swirly-Spagsonic (for eating spaghetti) turned Grandpa's wallpaper into confetti.

The Beard-tastic had Grandpa
near perfectly styled . . .

Till the foam overflowed,
and the clippers went **WILD.**

Well, Izabelle, who was so clever and bright,
would get rather cross when things didn't go right.
And she huffed, **"It's a duff! I've had it! I quit."**

She kicked her invention –
and called it a **"TWIT!"**

Izabelle fumed.

Grandpa smiled and chuckled.

"You can't give up just 'cos that thingy-bob buckled.
Now, trust me, young lady. Sometimes you need

to try again and again if you want to succeed."

Perhaps Grandpa was right, but still, Izabelle sighed.
She picked up her tool bag and wandered outside.

Kicking the stones on the path as she walked,
Izzy jumped at a **BUMP!**
Up ahead, something squawked.

From the clouds,
a poor crow had taken

a tumble,

and landed –

KAPOOOOOF!

– in a feathery jumble.

Izzy ran to the vet's. But the vet shook his head. "His wings are too broken to fix," the vet said.

"Perhaps take him home, and there you could try to teach him to live as a crow who . . . can't fly."

Day after day, Izzy thought she had found
something fun for her crow to do on the ground.

Like digging for worms,

and racing fat slugs,

hopscotch and hoopla,

and searching for bugs.

But the heartbroken crow simply gazed at the sky
as the other birds sang . . . and flew happily by.

One night, with the crow in the folds of her sweater,
Izzy sighed, "Oh, I WISH I could make him feel better.

I've tried. He won't play.

He won't drink.

He won't eat."

She was so very close to admitting defeat.

Grandpa said, "Izzy! Don't give up on him now.
I know you can do it. Just work out HOW!"

Then Grandpa passed Izzy her gadgety things . . .

And she knew what to do!
**"I'll invent some
NEW WINGS!"**

Izzy piled up her books,
and she started to read.

MACHINES

BIG BOOK of AERO DYNAMICS

UP THIS WAY

CIRCUITS AND WIRES

HOW TO CONNECT THEM WITHOUT CAUSING FIRES

Then she made a long list of the things she would need.

She searched for some batteries, and old electronics,
dismantled a mixer and the Swirly-Spagsonic.

The crow watched entranced and he held Izzy's drill,
while she bent, bashed and battered, and walloped until . . .

"Ta-Da!"

Izzy fastened the wings with a strap . . .

. . . but they hummed and they twitched, far too heavy to flap.

"AARGGHHH!" Izzy yelled.
"I'm no good at succeeding!"

The crow softly cawed,
his beady eyes pleading.

"What now?" Izzy sighed.
"Try AGAIN," Grandpa said.
"Okay, follow me!"
And with that, off she sped.

Izzy dived in a pond, where she borrowed a pump.

Then she took, from an engine, two sprockets, a sump.

Izzy fastened the wings.
They were light.
They were curvy.

But the wings, the wrong shape, turned the crow topsy-turvy!

"I give UP!"

Izzy yelled,
with a furious frown.

The crow sadly cawed,
as he hung upside down.

So, Izzy unscrewed the head from the shower,

found special circuits,
to adjust the wings' power . . .

And finally, using her trusty old pliers,
she borrowed the motors from two big blow-driers.

"Yes!" Izzy said. "The right shape, perfect weight . . ."

But ONE wing flapped madly.

The crow couldn't fly straight.

"I'VE HAD IT!" yelled Izzy, heading straight for a bin.
But the crow blocked her path. He just wouldn't give in.

Izzy twizzled and tinkered and, using his beak,
the tip-tapping crow gave the screws a good tweak.

Then he loosened the cog from Grandpa's old mixer . . .

"YOU CAN FLY!"

Izzy cried.

"Oh! Your name should be

Fixer!"

After two

loop the loops,

Fixer came into land . . .

And stood, happily cawing, upon Izzy's hand.
"You tried very hard," Grandpa said, "and succeeded!
You kept at it, Izzy you did what was needed."

"But don't pack your tools up,
your day's not quite ended.

A few things around here now need to be . . . MENDED!"

For Isabella Grace and Isabelle Bee xx - **PJ**
For Sita, Dani and Holger - **SO**

SIMON & SCHUSTER
First published in Great Britain in 2017 by Simon and Schuster UK Ltd
1st Floor, 222 Gray's Inn Road, London, WC1X 8HB • A CBS Company • Text copyright
© 2017 Pip Jones • Illustrations copyright © 2017 Sara Ogilvie • The right of Pip Jones
and Sara Ogilvie to be identified as the author and illustrator of this work has been
asserted by them in accordance with the Copyright, Designs and Patents Act, 1988
All rights reserved, including the right of reproduction in whole or in part in any form
A CIP catalogue record for this book is available from the British Library upon request
978-0-8570-7512-3 (HB) • 978-0-8570-7513-0 (PB) • 978-1-4711-5823-0 (eBook)
Printed in China • 10 9 8 7 6 5 4 3